BOOKCON
Carry-On

BOOKCON CARRY-ON
Library of Congress Control Number: 2025927910
ISBN: 979-8-9886879-6-2 (ebook)
ISBN: 979-8-9886879-7-9 (trade paperback)

First U.S. Edition
Published in the United States of America
Book designed by Robin Alvarez

BOOKCON

Carry-On

CONTENT WARNING

This book contains explicit sexual content and unapologetic explorations of desire.

To
Melanie Schubert

Thank you for bringing out
the sentient object lover in me.

ONE

I CHEWED on the inside of my cheek and checked the speedometer for the fifth time in sixty seconds. Happy as I was that my nineteen-year-old son would never drive over the speed limit, his need to uphold the laws of the road, no matter how late his mother was for her flight, was killing me.

We'd left early for the airport, too. But there was no way I could have predicted a big rig carrying sex toys would burst open on the freeway, sending cargo tumbling onto traffic. That made for an awkward few minutes, with my son carefully weaving around boxes of blow-up dolls and butt plugs. Little did he know what his own mother had planned during her *big* weekend trip.

"Hey, Victoria, you hot mama, take exit 101 toward Roseville International," the deep, suggestive voice of my car's GPS cooed. Whenever I drove alone, I called him Ramón, and pretended he was some hot, Latino model that had gotten himself stuck inside my dashboard. Ramón was happy to be there, of course, just so he could make sure I got to my destination safely.

My son Carlos scoffed in disgust. "As soon as you leave, I'm changing this thing back to its factory default."

"Don't you dare. I won't know how to turn him back on again." One of my best friends, Yazmine, uploaded Ramón the last time she came to visit—just after I signed my divorce papers. She said I needed to be reminded that I was a baddie every day, even if it was from a bot.

"Hey, Victoria, you sexy thang, take this exit."

Carlos grumbled to himself but flicked the blinker on. He looked over his shoulder twice before entering the off-ramp.

My knees started to bob. I gripped the worn paperback of *Warrior Lovers* to ease the building tension. I planned to reread it on the flight but didn't have the time to stuff it into my carry-on. The rational part of my mind told me stressing over my flight would do me no good. But I was worried about missing the only departure offered that day from my tiny airport in Northern California to Atlanta where I was meeting my best friends at Flirty Flings BookCon.

Like many bookstagrammers, Yazmine, Katie, and I had met online during the pandemic when we kept commenting on the same book review posts. We loved most of the same romances —hated several of the same ones, too. Eventually, our comment section banter turned into a group chat. Our conversations morphed into subjects beyond books. A deep and beautiful friendship was born, and at some point, we became like family.

"Mom," Carlos said.

He glanced at me like he was gauging the temperature of my mood based on how I answered back. He always did that.

"Yes?" I replied evenly. I didn't want him to feel my anxiety.

"Did Dad tell you what's going on this weekend?" he asked.

My stomach dropped. Not because I cared that my ex-husband, Alanzo, and his fiancée were having an engagement party, but because Carlos thought I cared.

"He did. And I'm happy for him." I wasn't. Why should this

new woman, pleasant and good with the kids as she was, get the best version of Alanzo? The version I built. The version I carried through sleepless nights with newborns, and raising three active boys, and job offers, and layoffs, and the loss of his parents, and so much more. I was Alanzo's support system for so long—since high school. But that wasn't all I was.

I had somehow let myself become whatever he wanted me to be. I became *his* lover. *His* wife. *His* whatever he needed at that moment. He was never mine. We were never a *we*. Everything had been about him and his needs, and I'd been too caught up in believing that lie to see the truth.

When our marriage ended, I was devastated. I thought my world was ending. But it wasn't because I loved him; it was because I would miss him in my life. I didn't know who I was without him. I didn't know what I wanted for myself because he had given me those answers for so long.

"Have you thought about dating again?" Carlos asked. "Or like, talking to an actual man? Not Ramón." When I shot him a look, he rolled his eyes. "We all know you named the GPS Ramón. Aren't you tired of reading about people in love?" He nodded toward the book I was clutching. "Don't you want a real man in your life?"

"Hell no. I had one for twenty-four years . . ." *and he ruined me*—was what I almost said. But I would never. I was a child of divorce. I knew the sinking feeling you got when your parents spoke poorly about each other. Beyond our shit, Alanzo had been a good father to our three children.

I understood why my son was asking me about finding someone new, someone real. Of my three boys, Carlos had always been the most sensitive, the one who saw everything for what it truly was. He tipped the scales when it came to empathy.

I changed the subject by pointing at a spot in the departure drop-off lane that he could pull into. "There."

"I know, Mom."

We slid to a smooth stop, and I hopped out at once. I grabbed my suitcase and carry-on from the backseat. As I stuffed my book inside my bag, I met my eldest son's expectant gaze.

"Are you sure you don't mind me leaving?" I asked. "You're only in town from school so often."

He shook his head and smiled, the gesture so like his dad. All three of my boys inherited Alanzo's handsome face and stocky builds, but they had my light brown skin and brown, wavy hair. "I see you like every other weekend," he said. "And we're staying at Dad's anyway."

"Right. Of course." I offered a tight smile.

"Have fun. Use those dating apps me and Katie loaded while you're there. I bet there's some nice old dudes where you're going."

"Old dudes? I'm forty-five!"

"Exactly."

I shut the door on his laughter.

"Love you!" I shouted through the window. "Don't forget your brothers have lacrosse in the morning!" His dad would be busy with preparations for his engagement party. We'd already made sure my mom and Carlos were okay with taking the twins to their game.

My son nodded and waved before putting on his blinker, checking his blind spots, and driving off.

My phone buzzed. I dug into my pants and winced at the message on my screen.

> Hello, Happy Skies customer. Please make your way to Gate 15B. Your flight will be boarding in 30 minutes.

"Shit!" I grabbed my bags and sprinted inside.

TWO

SUITCASE CHECKED at the front counter and ticket in hand, I ran up the escalator and to the TSA checkpoint. The line wasn't long, Roseville International was the smallest of all international airports in my state, but I didn't have a moment to spare. I wove through the ropes that made up the security line. The queue was moving fast. *Thank goodness.*

A buzz tickled my hip.

I took out my phone. The screen was black. I blinked and looked around when the vibrating continued. None of the passengers near me seemed to be getting a call. The buzzing grew louder. Where in the hell was that sound coming from? I tilted my head and frowned down at my overstuffed carry-on.

"Oh no," I whispered.

The whirring was coming from inside the bag.

"Next!" one of the TSA agents called.

There were just two people in front of me now.

I slapped the fancy weekend bag I'd splurged on as hard as I could without causing a scene, and the buzzing grew even louder. Only one thing in my carry-on would make that sound. My neck went hot.

Fucking hell.

I *knew* I should have put the girthy vibrator in my checked luggage, but it was stuffed with the books I wanted to get signed by my favorite authors and the costume I planned on

wearing to the book con after party. Besides, my youngest had helped me pack, so there was no way I was going to put it inside there.

"Over here, ma'am," the agent ordered.

I shook my bag violently, willing the girthy vibrator inside to stop.

"Ma'am?"

The vibrating grew louder.

Why is it that whenever you're in a rush, the most annoying shit happens?

"Ma'am!" the agent barked.

Someone tapped me on the shoulder. I whipped my head around to face the person behind me. It was the cutest old man with wisps of white hair sprouting from his head. Now *this* was an old man. The men on my dating apps were simply men. Not *old dudes*, I told myself soothingly.

"They're calling you," he said.

"Me?" I whirled toward the front of the queue, realizing I was the "ma'am." I certainly didn't feel like a ma'am. I felt like a miss. Like a hot, young thing, with perky breasts and zero fine lines whiskering her eyes. My mind was generously delusional in that way.

"Hurry up, lady," someone grumbled.

I adjusted my still-vibrating carry-on and shuffled forward. The TSA agent blinked at me from over her cat-eye glasses, but let me through. I placed my bag and purse on the conveyor belt and sent a silent prayer to the heavens that my vibrator would shut the fuck up.

Once through the metal detectors, I rushed forward to spy

on the thick-mustached TSA agent standing behind the X-ray machine. Two bags passed inspection with little fuss. Now it was my turn.

Wincing, I observed my leather bag worm through the X-ray machine.

Buzzzzzzzzzzzz.

The vibrations rumbling from my newly purchased dildo grew so loud, I felt it in my stomach. From the raised eyebrows and curious glances cast about, I was sure everyone around me felt it, too.

The thick-mustached agent retrieved my bag from the conveyor belt. Horrified, I stood there, feeling all eyes turn toward my carry-on. The agent took hold of the walkie talkie hanging on his shoulder and whispered something into it.

"No," I groaned. My cheeks grew flushed. I wiped my sweating palms on my jeans. This poor agent probably thought there was some sort of weapon inside. I mean, it *could* be used as a weapon, if need be. It was extra-large and hard as a rod.

Two agents left their positions at the metal detectors to join him. A third stormed forward, readjusting his belt. He had that harried, bloodshot look that people who took their jobs way too seriously seemed to always sport.

"Everyone, stand back!" he shouted.

Yup. I was right. This man was serious about his duties.

The other agents looked at each other and pressed their lips together to hold back their laughter.

"Whose bag is this?" the harried agent barked.

A dozen thoughts sprinted through my mind. *I should just run. Turn around and find the nearest exit and never fly or leave my home ever again. Or pretend to faint. Cause a distraction. No, even better—I should pretend I was appalled like someone had played a trick on me.*

"Whose bag is this?" he bellowed for the entire damn airport to hear.

Was it really that serious? They could see the dildo on the X-ray. Surely they knew the shape of a dick and balls when they saw one. Now they were causing a scene far bigger than my dildo, and everyone was staring. I wanted to melt into the floor.

As if caught in slow motion, one of the agents, a tall young man with an American flag pin on his collar, plucked at that fucking bright pink luggage tag I just had to have. I never traveled, which was why I got a little too excited and bought every accessory I thought I needed.

"Victoria Lopez! Which one of you is Victoria Lopez?"

I closed my eyes. This was it. My life was over. I was now going to become some GIF on the internet. Shaking, I raised my hand.

"What is making this sound?" the harried agent snarled at me.

The other agents snickered. They knew exactly what lay inside. My ears flamed. They were enjoying this. They probably didn't even care about the dildo. They must have been trying to get a rise out of this agent, but I was the one caught in the crossfire.

"Ma'am!" the agent called.

There was that damn word again.

I shuffled to the glass wall standing as a barrier between us. I held my head low, trying to hide my face behind my hair.

"It's my vibrator," I whispered.

"What?" he yelled. "Speak up!"

"It's . . . it's . . . it's my dildo."

The harried man's jaw dropped. One of the agents behind him snorted. We were off to the side of the line now, but, with so many agents hovering over my things, the TSA queues were backing up. I shrank into myself as much as possible.

The tall agent nudged the harried man with his elbow. "You better check what's inside. Just to be safe."

"I do always say it's better to be safe than sorry," he agreed.

Like a doctor on TV, he stretched latex gloves over his fingers with a snap. He unzipped the bag slowly as if it were an actual explosive device. I gulped. There, vibrating on top of my makeup bag, lay the lifelike dick of my dreams, still secured inside its clear packaging. The buzzing whirred louder. The balls at the base undulated with a mechanical hum as if the universe wasn't quite satisfied with the depth of my shame.

"Good *God*," a tiny grandma gawked beside me.

A father shielded his child's eyes.

And the harried agent just stood there staring like he'd unearthed Pandora's box.

I didn't have any minutes to spare, and the crowd was growing.

"May I try to turn it off?" I asked, but I didn't give him time to answer. I rushed around the glass and snatched my prized dildo. It was heavier than I remembered. Thicker, too. I don't know what I was thinking buying this. I hadn't had sex in three years. Did I really believe I could handle something so meaty?

Shakily, I tore the bottom of the packaging open and tried

the switch tucked away on the underside of the balls. To my confusion, the dildo wouldn't stop. I pushed it again and again.

My phone, still inside the bin along with my purse, lit up with a notification.

> Hello, Happy Skies customer. Please make your way to Gate 15B. Your flight is boarding.

Cursing, I tried smacking the long shaft against my palm.

"Can't you take the batteries out or something?" the harried agent asked, his face a mix of horrified and mesmerized by the size of the cock in my grasp.

"It doesn't have batteries!" I cried. "It's rechargeable."

I slapped the dildo harder, and the guards winced, unconsciously shifting their crotches away like they experienced phantom assaults.

A young person pulled out her phone and looked into her screen. "Oh my god, guys, I had to go live because you'd never believe what's happening." She pointed the camera at me, not even trying to be sneaky about it.

I whipped my face away.

"It . . . it won't turn off," I hissed to the agent.

The agent opened his mouth to offer advice, but the intercom crackled to life.

"Victoria Lopez. Victoria Lopez. Please make your way to Gate 15B. All other passengers have boarded the flight, and doors will be closing shortly."

I squirmed. "That's me."

"I'm sorry, ma'am, but I can't let you take this *thing* on the flight without consulting my manager. What if it overheats?

What if it explodes? It will just take a few minutes for her to get here."

I almost started to cry right then and there. Because I was humiliated. Because I knew phone cameras were pointed in my direction. Because I was so looking forward to alone time in my hotel room the next three days with my king-size dildo and king-size bed.

Alas, I had to make this decision or risk missing my flight.

I grabbed my prized dick and chucked it into the garbage. The buzzing amplified, thumping against the plastic walls of the rubbish bin in protest. Frat bros howled with laughter. Now the tears really did start to come.

The thick-mustached TSA agent who had originally flagged my bag offered me a sympathetic grimace. He silently closed the zipper and grabbed the blue receiver near the X-ray screen.

"Attention Gate 15B," his voice blared through the speakers. "Victoria Lopez is coming."

I mouthed my thanks and set off at a sprint.

My tears quickly dried, and mortification turned into a deep and consuming sort of disappointment. Because I might be coming to Gate 15B, but I knew that I wouldn't be *coming* the way I really wanted this weekend.

And it had been far too long.

THREE

"YOU'RE FUCKING KIDDING ME!" Katie exclaimed as she spooned cheesecake into her mouth.

Yazmine, who dubbed herself the third tip of our triangle of friendship, stood at the foot of my bed, mouth agape.

I set my empty wine glass on the bedside table and unsheathed a fork from a paper napkin.

"I wish I was kidding," I said.

I stabbed into the decadent dessert we'd splurged on from room service. I didn't care about the contemptible price. This bed-top picnic in my hotel room was what I deserved after what happened at the airport.

"I bet if you look up *buzzing airport shlong* on TikTok right now you'd see my horrified face," I grumbled.

Katie pressed her lips together to keep from laughing. The movement sent the salmon sperm-infused mask she was wearing sliding down her delicate face.

"Just how big was it?" Yazmine flung her long black braid over her shoulder before filling her own glass with the boxed wine she'd procured.

"*Big*. Big." I cupped my hands together around the phantom width of a large plantain to prove the girth of my tragic vibrator.

"Damn, girl," Yazmine said. "You really were planning on letting loose this trip."

"It's been over three years since I had . . . *fun*."

"Three years?" Katie repeated.

"Alanzo was never in the mood toward the end of our relationship. No surprise there. And I wasn't in the mood after the divorce. Plus, I'm still sleeping in the same bed we shared. The twins are always running in and out of my room. They're fifteen but the way they shriek and play-fight, you'd think they were still toddlers. So, coming here, having a room all to myself, I thought this would be my time to shine."

Katie gasped. "I have an idea." She put her spoon down and clapped her hands. "Why don't we catch an Uber and go to a sex shop!"

Yazmine brightened at the prospect. Shopping, especially for naughty toys, was one of her favorite hobbies. She grabbed her phone and started typing frantically onto the screen.

I shook my head. "I think I'm dildoed out for the day. I'm honestly exhausted from traveling across the country to see your asses." I plopped back on my pillows. "I'm not the party animal I once was."

"Yeah, well, old age will do that to you," Yazmine said.

"Only if you let it." Katie tapped her temple. "It's all in the mind."

"My mind has had enough. Let's call it an early night," I suggested, already feeling my eyelids growing heavy from the red wine. "The opening keynote is at nine in the morning, and we'll basically be going hard the rest of the day. Then there's the costume party after—might as well rest up."

Yazmine clicked her tongue. "Take one giant dildo away and she's suddenly too tired to have any excitement."

I snorted. "I'm sure I'll have plenty of excitement in my sleep. I'll be dreaming of giant dildos chasing me through the airport for the rest of my life."

"It can't be *that* bad," Yazmine offered.

"A girl went live and recorded the whole thing," I deadpanned.

"She probably has a small following." Katie scrolled on her phone. "I'm sure no one has seen . . ." She clapped a hand over her mouth.

My stomach dipped.

Yazmine plopped onto the bed beside Katie, and her jaw dropped. The girls looked at me, then at the screen, then at me again. Shock and awe battled for dominance across their expressions.

"See? It *is* that bad!" I complained. "I can never show my face at the kids' school again."

"It's not that bad. I promise." Katie flipped the screen toward me.

Relief flooded my body at once. The clip did show me, but it was of my side profile, and my hair was covering most of my face.

"Turn up the volume," Yazmine ordered.

Katie did, and the video replayed. I watched a panicked version of myself flinging that veiny dick-imposter into the trash. Someone had dubbed over the original audio with the sound of a scoreboard buzzer going off and an imaginary crowd going wild. I snorted, which gave the girls the last bit of approval they needed to lose control. I couldn't even describe the sounds coming from my friends as laughter. It was more like two hyenas cackling.

With a chuckle, I clicked on the search bar and a few other videos popped up from different angles. My face was a little distorted in each one. There were comments from women cheering me on for even trying to bring something on board that was meant to bring me pleasure. The more I watched, the more I found myself not caring if I was seen or not. Sure, my boys would be horrified, but that was life. I wasn't *only* a mom. I wasn't *only* someone's ex-wife. I was a woman who had needs. There wasn't anything wrong with that. Was the situation hilariously embarrassing? Absolutely. But oh fucking well.

Laughter bubbled up and out of me. I cackled with my girls until I got a stitch in my side.

When we were spent, I swiped at the joy-filled tears gathering at the corners of my eyes. "I'd gladly endure that again to be here with you two."

Yazmine, Katie, and I had planned on going to this very book convention two years ago to finally see each other in real life. But Alanzo had other plans. Plans—meaning one of the moms in my neighborhood walking group. She'd gotten the time and date of me leaving all wrong and showed up at my back door wearing nothing but a hideous peacoat.

Instead of meeting me for the first time in this very hotel, surrounded by books and authors we adored, Yazmine and Katie found me hunched over on the floor in my half-empty bedroom closet. My friends picked me up and cleaned my house and fed my children while I sobbed all the pain away.

It wasn't that I was so shocked by him cheating, or that I thought our marriage was even good. We hadn't had sex in a year by then. But I had thought he cared enough about me as a human being, as the mother of his children, to end our marriage with some dignity.

Now, he was getting remarried. At least it wasn't to the bitch that I once thought of as a friend. Alanzo looked happy. He looked loved—more than I had loved him since the boys came. I had loved him once . . . We were high school sweethearts, and I used to think he was my everything. But our passion died slowly. It wasn't a knife to the back that killed us—it was the gangrene. Dozens of small cuts left untreated and festering over the years until there was nothing but a rotting shell. A front that made sure no one in our lives saw what was actually going on.

To everyone around us, we were the perfect pair. He was the head of our household. Always out and about. Always charming anyone he met at the office, the gym, the kids' school, or on the golf course. When he'd invite people over, sometimes without even telling me, our home was perfectly clean and meals were hot on the stove. I did my best to make him look as good as he wanted, to do anything he wanted, because that's exactly what his mother had done for his father.

The worst part of our marriage, though, was the fact that I had let him convince me that I was the one always in the wrong. When we were in bed, alone, he had to be the one calling all the shots as if my sexual needs were an assault to his manliness. I prioritized his delicate ego and insecurities over myself. I gave up trying, and our lovemaking—if that was even what I could call it—became a chore rather than a release.

I looked at Katie, who would never go without dick for three years. Then at Yazmine, who was very vocal about the importance of having her needs satisfied by the woman she was dating or one of her many toys. A long sigh slipped out of me. I should have cared for myself that way, too. But I thought Alanzo's needs were more important. That made me feel sick for myself.

I deserved someone who fought tooth and nail for my happiness; someone who was brave enough to let me lead. I needed a warrior—valiant and strong and full of honor. Instead, I got a damn dog.

Yazmine squeezed my thigh and offered a warm smile. "You're right. We should take it easy tonight."

"After we finish this cheesecake," Katie added.

I sat back up and grabbed my empty glass. "And the box of wine."

CLANGING bells blared in my eardrums. Groaning, I burrowed my head under the pillow, but the bells persisted. In the groggy recesses of my mind, I remembered my vibrator. Remembered the constant buzzing and that horrified TSA agent.

I shot up.

The room spun in sickening circles. I grimaced and pinched the bridge of my nose.

"Turn your alarm off," Yazmine moaned. She lay sprawled at the foot of my bed. Katie, unsurprisingly, had made a nest for herself on the floor. She had the energy and sleeping habits of a squirrel.

My alarm continued to scream. I searched through blankets, pillows, and color-coded Excel sheets Katie and Yazmine made that mapped out every author, vendor, and panel we wanted to see until I found my phone. After I hit stop, I checked the time. Wincing, I bent over and slapped Yazmine on her bubbly ass.

"Hey," she said, her voice muffled by the pillow her nose was buried in.

"It's eight. Time to get ready for the best day of our lives. You two need to go to your room and shower. I can smell the wine oozing out of your pores from here."

Katie's head shot up. "Oh my god. It's really happening. We get to see all our favorite authors in one place!" She scrambled up and snatched the crumpled spreadsheets from my bed.

She bounced up and twirled in a circle. "Get your asses ready, girls, we're finally doing this!"

FOUR

BOOK CARTS TRAILING BEHIND US, we entered a bookworm's paradise. According to the map Katie printed, this was the largest of the three ballrooms. There were 169 authors in attendance this year, and each one had tables filled with special editions to purchase, character art, and stickers for their readers.

My girls and I went from table to table, getting the books we'd buddy read together signed first. We joked with the authors and quoted our favorite lines back to them. We talked to other readers while in line and gossiped over publishing tea. Truly, it was the most fun I'd had in a good long while. And possibly the most money I'd spent on myself ever. After I purchased a rabbit shifter novella where the bunny had more abs than Miles Teller in Top Gun, a bit of guilt clawed up my spine.

I didn't really need that book. I didn't need any of the little trinkets or that crochet vagina. This extra money could have been used to buy the boys something nice. And what about this trip? I probably should have spent this weekend with my kids. What if they needed me during this strange transition in their lives? What if the twins forgot to pack their lacrosse uniforms again?

No. I stuffed the worry and guilt down. My boys were old enough to take care of themselves. Let Alanzo worry about

"

uniforms for a change, even if his engagement party was later this evening.

Should I text him just in case?

I pulled out my phone but stopped myself. This had been one of Alanzo's biggest complaints about me during our relationship. He said I pestered him too much. That I got on his case about bills and dishes and putting his dirty clothes in the hamper.

It enraged me to no end.

Why couldn't he just *do* those things? Why did he force me to put down my role as wife and take up the mantle of manager?

But honestly, I was a damn good manager. I kept all four of the men in my life in line. I wondered if that was why it irritated Alanzo so much. Maybe he hated not being the one calling all the shots. He was certainly like that during sex—*when* we'd had sex.

Who cared now? He was his future wife's problem.

My phone buzzed. A picture of the twins in their uniforms popped onto the screen.

CARLOS

Don't worry, Mom. Got these dorks dressed and to the game on time.

My heart swelled with pride. But it hurt, too. I hadn't been in a different state from them ever in their lives. What if they wanted me to call them and wish them luck but didn't want to bother me?

Yazmine and Katie pulled out the books for the next signing.

Like a bewildered ghost, I floated behind them, my thumb hovering over my phone.

"Go call the boys," Yazmine deadpanned.

"I'm sure they're fine." I waved my phone in dismissal but didn't put it away.

"They are. But you're not. Call them." She held out her hand. "I'll get your book signed and personalized for you."

"Are you sure?"

Katie took my cart. "Go. But don't forget we're going to see your favorite narrator next. I saw him post about giving away free penis pens."

"Too bad they aren't life-sized," I grumbled.

"From the looks of things, you wanted something larger than life." Yazmine wiggled her brows.

The girls' giggles trailed after me as I headed toward the door. I pulled up Carlos's number when I heard someone call my name.

Victoria.

I stopped.

My jaw dropped, because the person calling me sounded exactly like Marcos Medina—my favorite audiobook narrator. The very person we were supposed to visit next, according to the girls' itinerary.

I didn't turn around, because why in the hell would Marcos Medina be calling my name?

Victoria.

There could have been a dozen other Victorias here. But just in case, I casually peeked over my shoulder. My posture slumped. It wasn't Marcos. He was at his table signing copies of his most recent audiobook narration, *Sentient Sex*.

Victoria, Marcos's voice sounded like it was right beside me —impossibly, because he currently was talking to a man sporting a *Banned Books Are Sexy* shirt. *Victoria. Over here.*

I whirled around and found myself standing in front of a table laden with the hottest and most exquisitely detailed artwork I'd ever seen. There were ethereal fae with golden headpieces and broody vampires with blood trickling down their bare chests. *Sexy* bare chests. Another print was of a gorgeous woman with a pointy witch hat and curves for days. Her sultry eyes followed me when I turned my face side to side.

Toward the rear of the table sat the artist's more salacious prints. Sex scenes. Fingering. Fellatio. The works. Each scene was hotter than the next. One was of two jacked men kissing while jerking each other off. Another was of a woman getting rammed by a centaur. The look on her face screamed of pleasure and pain. I found myself biting my own lip. I wished I could remember what that sort of climax felt like, but how could I? Alanzo's dick was far from resembling anything centaurian.

Victoria.

My head snapped toward the end of the table. Small figurines stood immobile like an army frozen in time. I peered around the table to see if there was someone pranking me behind it, but there was no one there. The saleswoman was standing on the opposite side, helping a shopper pay for her goodies. The customer's cheeks were pink, and she was grinning from ear to ear. I could see why. The print she purchased was of a woman floating in the air. The grim reaper himself had her in his grasp, and he was pleasuring her with the hilt of his scythe.

Holy hell.

I returned my focus to finding whoever kept calling my name. A few volunteers were unpacking boxes nearby. They were too busy chattering over the merch inside to even notice me. There wasn't anyone around that would match the tone of this person's voice.

With a sigh, I stepped back. I must have been hearing things. Or, more likely, I was still half-drunk from all the wine we consumed last night.

I'm right here, Victoria. Look down, my queen.

I jolted. My gaze landed on the figurines once more. Some of them were the 3D versions of the characters in the art prints. Some were altogether different. There were mermen and female knights with rounded breastplates. There were pirates, and deities, and all sorts of ripped monsters. Whoever made these little statues was incredibly talented. Each one was so unique and utterly lifelike. I was in awe.

One of the figurines stood at the very front. He was striking. A Mexica warrior in his battle regalia. I'd studied Mesoamerican history for a bit when I wanted to learn more about my own roots. The jaguar mask he sported told me that he was high-ranking amongst his people. My eyes trailed down his torso, to the tight V that disappeared beneath his beautifully made maxtlatl. The artist even painted a jaguar design on the loincloth he wore.

"Do you like him?"

I jumped. I hadn't realized the saleswoman was finished

ringing up her customer. She smiled at me with an open warmth. A diamond glinted from her incisor and her winged liner accentuated her siren-green eyes. Her skin was a warm brown and covered in what seemed to be the most random tattoos. I instantly liked her.

"He's magnificent," I said. "Did the artist hand sculpt these?"

"I did. With the help of a bit of magic." She winked.

"I believe it. These are *so* lifelike. You're incredibly talented." I bent down and took a closer look at the warrior. His thighs were a work of wonder. Thick and cut with muscle. Built for speed. For jumping. For thrusting. I could only imagine what he could do to me if he were real.

"Does that one speak your name?" she asked.

Speak my name? That was a specific word choice.

My pulse sped up as I let my thoughts roam to a world where he and I were alone and naked under a starry sky.

We could make that happen, that sexy voice whispered into my ear.

I jolted.

"Is something wrong?" the woman asked.

The stimulating voice came again: *The only thing wrong is us not being together. Take me, Victoria. Take me and I will serve your every need.*

Well, that was it then. I had officially lost my mind. Because that fucking toy was talking to me. His lips didn't move, but I knew it was him. And the worst part? His voice alone made my nipples hard.

"How . . ." I cleared my throat. "How much is he?"

"They aren't for sale, unfortunately," she said.

"Oh." Disappointment dripped inside me. I wasn't even sure why. He was just a figurine. Nothing more.

She gestured toward the dozen or so statues. "These effigies are one of a kind. I am their guardian of sorts. I cannot let them be taken by just anyone. It is up to them who they go to."

"Effigies? Doesn't that mean these figurines were sculpted to look like someone in real life?"

Maybe I could look up whoever this warrior was. If she based him off a model, I could . . . what, exactly? Masturbate to his pic? With what? My damn dildo had been taken by TSA. Technically, I flung it in the trash, but close enough. I guess I could try to get myself off, but that didn't seem nearly as fun as having my airport shlong.

The artist's eyes sparkled with knowing. "All of these beauties carry the spirit of someone who once walked among the land of the living—either in this realm or in another. These souls didn't find their true purpose in their time and have come back to fulfill it."

"I see." I didn't. But she gave off eccentric artist vibes, so maybe I wasn't cool enough to understand. Maybe she was a witch, here to grant wishes. Or maybe it was all from some fantasy book that I'd yet to read. Either way, the effigy was not for sale.

I wiggled my phone. "I need to make a call, but I'll bring my friends around, and I'm sure we'll purchase some art prints."

She held out her hand to stop me. "Are you sure you didn't hear any of these pieces speaking to you?"

There she went again, talking about one of them speaking

to me. Did she hear someone call my name too? I frowned. She didn't even know my name. How would she know if someone was calling it?

I shook my head. Thoroughly confused.

Take me, Victoria. Let me be your warrior. Let me rescue you.

I sucked in a breath. The voice sent chills crawling up my spine. It was too real. Too close. It made my skin too hot.

"I need some fresh air." I reached over the effigies and took her business card. *BookCon Carry-On* was the name of her company. My cheeks flamed. I didn't even want to think about carry-ons right now. On the back of the card, just above a QR code, it stated: *Now You Can Bring Your Book Boyfriend with You Anywhere You Go.*

"What a fun concept," I said. "See you later."

Before she could say another word, I dashed across the room. My palm pressed on the door, and I shoved it open. As I exited the bustling ballroom, I swore I heard that baritone voice call out my name once more.

FIVE

CARLOS PICKED up the phone on the fourth ring.

"Hey, Mom." His tone was clipped, on edge. He was mad at me. I just knew it. Angry that I'd chosen Flirty Flings BookCon over him on such a big weekend.

My spine stiffened. "What's wrong?"

"These damn refs keep penalizing our team!" In the background, irate families booed. Lacrosse parents were the worst. Or best. Depending on who was on your side.

"What's the score?"

"Zero. Zero. Because of the fucking refs!"

I winced and yanked the blaring phone away from my ear.

"Language," I snapped. Though, it was more out of habit. Carlos was old enough to do whatever he wanted. Plus, those fucking refs *were* annoying.

"Why is everything so quiet? Aren't you supposed to be with Yaz and Katie?"

I'd tucked myself away from the busy corridor where the three ballrooms emptied out to.

"I needed to use the restroom and figured I'd check in on you guys." If I went to the bathroom after our conversation, then this wouldn't be a lie. But I had to say something. I didn't want to sound desperate. Or to make him think I was spending my entire vacation worrying about him and his brothers instead of having a good time.

"We're fine, Mom. The boys are kicking ass. Well, sort of. We'll FaceTime you later. Go have fun. I'm begging you."

"I *am* having fun."

"Mmm-hmm."

"I am!"

"Good. You deserve it. Tell Yaz she owes me 20 bucks."

"For what?"

"We had a bet to see how soon you'd call today. She said you'd call right away, but I said you'd try to hold off and let us have our space. I win."

I scoffed noisily. At that very moment a random woman walked by. She threw an offended glance my way. I held up the phone and mouthed, "My son." Her face morphed with understanding. She wiggled her phone in silent camaraderie.

"I'm going to hang up, Mom. Grandma Mary just bought nachos from the concession stand."

"*Nachos*? It's like 9 am there."

"Is there a wrong time to eat nachos?"

"Well . . . no . . . but—"

"Gotta go. Love you!"

The line went dead.

I sighed and leaned against the wall. It certainly didn't seem like the kids were too worried about me or mad that I left. Besides, my mom was there, which meant they were going to be well fed and spoiled rotten.

I fidgeted with the hem of my shirt. Everyone was fine.

Everyone but me.

It seemed like everyone's lives were moving on. My ex was remarrying. Carlos was loving college life. The twins were like two tornadoes tearing through my house at random. Everyone was in a constant state of forward motion but me. I lived in the same house. I slept in the same bed. Hell, I hadn't even bought new underwear in who knew how long.

When I did try to switch things up, I ended up going viral.

A text brightened my screen.

KATIE

We're about to meet Marcos Medina now!
Where are you?!

Marcos Medina's honeyed voice played in my mind.

And then I thought about that damn doll.

I took the business card out of my pocket and scanned the QR code under the description. Reviews for *BookCon Carry-On* filled my screen. Every single review was five stars.

⭐⭐⭐⭐⭐ OMFG. My life is forever changed.

⭐⭐⭐⭐⭐ My legs have been quivering for weeks!

⭐⭐⭐⭐⭐ IF I COULD GIVE MY EXPERI-
ENCE(S) SIXTY-NINE STARS I WOULD.

⭐⭐⭐⭐⭐ Thank the Gods I listened when I heard my name called.

My spine straightened. When they heard their name called? This was getting too strange.

A text banner popped up on the top of my screen.

YAZMINE

Bitch. Where are you?

I winced and raced back into the ballroom. I took a sharp right and all but sprinted to meet the girls who were giggling at the front of Marcos Medina's line.

"There she is!" Katie exclaimed. "Marcos, this is your biggest fan, Victoria."

"Well, hello, Victoria," he crooned.

I had been wrong. The voice calling my name sounded nothing like Marcos's. The voice whispering my name was *so* much sexier.

"Your friends have told me all about you," Marcos teased.

I shimmied, enjoying the attention for what it was, a bit of fun. "I bet they did."

With an overconfident grin, Marcos rested an elbow on the table and recited my favorite line—everyone's favorite line—from *Sentient Sex*: "Did you come here for me, or are you here so I can make *you* come?"

We all laughed and clapped, cheering Marcos on. But in the back of my mind, I was thinking about one thing. Going back to BookCon Carry-On.

SIX

WITH COPIES of *Sentient Sex* signed and carefully put back inside our book carts, I dragged the girls to the other side of the ballroom.

"We have two minutes to spare and then we have to get in line for the first panel of the day," Katie instructed.

"Fine by me," I said. "I just want to see something for a sec."

See if I was losing my mind, or if they heard it too.

We wove through a horde of readers waiting for ARC drops. My heart plunged when I spotted BookCon Carry-On. The table had been cleared away.

A sign had been left on top of the black linen.

Sorry for the inconvenience but I had to close early today. Will be back bright and early tomorrow morning.

I blinked when I saw an additional note left on the bottom corner.

For Victoria Lopez.

She knew my name. My whole-ass name.

Someone wished to stay behind for you. He's waiting under the table.

Enjoy. :)

"Someone is under the table?" Yazmine asked.

I didn't answer. My heart was beating too fast in my chest, and I had no clue why. I dropped to one knee and pulled the cloth up. There, tucked away in the shadows, was the Mexica warrior.

Someone wished to stay behind for you. Huh. What had the artist said to me earlier? "It is up to them who they go to."

I, apparently, had been chosen.

Another note waited for me near the base of his feet. I plucked it up and read it.

Now you can bring the book boyfriend of your dreams to life.

Directions: For a lover so remarkable you'd swear he was pulled right out of a fairy tale, simply give this effigy a lick.

You won't be sorry.

I stuffed the note into my pocket. There was no way I was going to lick some toy given to me by a stranger, but I reached for him hungrily. The second my fingers wrapped around his body, an electrifying jolt shot through me. The sensation burrowed right into my most sensitive place. I gasped. Completely and utterly turned on. My thumb roamed over the effigy. It was strangely warm. And it didn't feel toy-like as I'd imagined. He felt almost like my dildo. Soft and skin-like on the outside and firm on the inside.

Heat pulsed at the base of my pelvis as I drew my thumb up and down his torso. His loincloth was made from actual fabric. I'd been so wrong in thinking the entire thing was constructed of clay. How strange. I thought he was one solid piece before. I wondered what lay beneath the fabric wrapped snugly around his slender hips. I started to lift it up when Katie's head popped in beside me.

I jumped. My head hit the underside of the table, and I nearly dropped him.

She gasped. "Are you okay?"

"I think so." Truth was, I had no idea if I was okay. Not because I hit my head—it wasn't hard enough to cause any worry—but because this doll was turning me on.

"What is that?" she asked.

I showed her the figurine.

Katie's head quirked to the side like a perplexed pup. "It's a doll? The shop owner just gave him to you?"

"The artist must have noticed how much I liked him."

"That was nice of her."

"For sure," I whispered, my thumb drawing circles over his pecs. His teeny nipples were hard as mine.

We stood, and I quickly showed Yazmine.

"He's hot," she said. "For a guy."

He really was though. Cheekbones as high as a cliff's edge. Strong brows hovering over deep-set, obsidian eyes. His jawline was cutting, and the veins running up his arms made me wet.

What the hell was wrong with me?

Yazmine placed her hand on my shoulder. "Do you need a break? You look flushed."

"A break?" Katie screeched. "Like hell she does. We have a panel to get to." She plucked the warrior from my grasp and gently placed him inside my book cart. "You sit there, stud." She faced us. "Let's go. I want a seat up front."

SEVEN

BY THE TIME we finished dinner, my feet were throbbing worse than if we'd been walking around Disneyland all day. But our evening wasn't finished yet. Tonight was the big party the con hosted for the guests. The theme was to come dressed as your alter ego. By trade I was a pediatric nurse. I wore teddy bear scrubs and earrings that correlated with whatever holiday season we were in. Tonight, there wasn't going to be a single wholesome thing about what I wore.

I laid my costume out on my bed and scrutinized every inch.

The sexy nurse outfit was perilously short. All my cellulite would be exposed and half my ass, too. But being here, with my friends, and among people who only judged you by the content in your book stack, I felt liberated.

No one was going to be looking at the dimples in my thighs anyway. All eyes would be on my breasts, which would be shoved up to the heavens. Yazmine always said they were one of my greatest assets so I might as well bless the world with them. Alanzo would have turned red in the face like a baby getting his first shots if he saw me like this when we were married. He would have told me I was an embarrassment of a wife and mother.

Even the way I dressed normally pissed him off.

He had loved my body in my tight jeans and low-cut shirts when we dated, but when we got married, everything changed.

He became possessive. Domineering. The body he loved became something he thought he owned. He didn't want me going out of our house unless my curves were hidden behind bulky sweaters.

What a loser. I couldn't believe I stayed with him for so long.

I grabbed my costume and started for the bathroom but stopped when I caught my reflection in the standing mirror. I'd always been thick naturally, always had more curves than I knew what to do with. What a shame that I'd wasted years of my life not being able to fully explore my wants and needs, and how to make myself come, all because I thought my body belonged to my husband. Maybe now it was time I learned.

Gazing at myself, I unzipped my pants and slowly drew them downward. I pulled my t-shirt over my head and took off my sports bra. My breasts hung freely, full and round, not exactly like they were when I was younger, but still alluring. My nipples perked from the chill of the whirring AC.

Slowly, timidly, I slid my hands over my stomach and toward my breasts. I cupped their heaviness within my grasp and ran my thumbs around my nipples. The tiniest pulse of need flared between my thighs.

Desperate to fan the flames of that delicious sensation, I imagined the Mexica warrior bursting into my room. His strong, calloused hands groping and kneading my breasts. His hot tongue lapping over my rock-hard nipples.

"Yes," I moaned to my imaginary lover.

One of my hands slid down the length of my body until I found the apex of my thighs. I was already slick with liquid heat at the thought of such a strong, lithe man desperate for me. I closed my eyes and groaned as I rubbed my clit, imagining his hot tongue doing the most devious things to me.

"Yes," I whispered, grinding against my own hand. "Yes."

Yes.

My eyes shot open. That third *yes* hadn't come from me.

I whirled around, my breasts jiggling.

"Who's there?" I asked.

But I was completely alone.

My stomach dipped to my toes when I noticed the warrior figurine standing on the desk. I sure as hell didn't put him there. I'd left him in the book cart before rushing out to meet the girls for dinner.

Frowning, I gave him a second look. His body was positioned differently than I remembered. When I first saw him, his fingers were wrapped around a spear and his other hand was flexed by his side. Now, that flexed hand had moved, and it clutched his thick dick through his loincloth. I blinked hard, willing my vision to find its way back to reality, yet his positioning remained.

"What in the actual hell?" I stepped closer to him. Maybe his arms were movable. Maybe one of the girls did this as a prank. My eyes slipped to the outline of his dick. It was huge for his size.

My phone buzzed on the bed. I yelped at the intrusion.

BOOK SLUTS GROUP CHAT

KATIE

Meet you at the rooftop bar in 15.

YAZMINE

It's closed for refurbishments, but the lobby bar is open. I'm here now.

I winced. I was absolutely going to be late.

My attention snapped back to the warrior. To my . . . relief? Confusion? Gratitude? The figurine's positioning had gone back to the way I remembered it.

Exhaling, I relaxed my shoulders. Apparently, my imagination was a bit too transportive. Katie always said I should try writing because of how good I was at making up scenarios in my head. Maybe she was onto something.

The clock on the bedside table blinked at me. Fourteen minutes until I needed to meet my girls. Maybe I could try to get myself off first? I didn't think I could. Besides, I hadn't had an orgasm in so damn long that I didn't want my first time diving back into the climax pool to be rushed.

I found myself in the mirror and winked.

"Don't worry, girl. You'll get yours somehow, someway this weekend."

I cleaned myself up and threw on a fresh coat of ruby red lipstick. When I had dressed, I sat on the bed, facing the warrior. His dark eyes watched me intently. God, I wished I had a life-size version of him in my room at that very moment. I didn't want a new man in my life. I wasn't sure if I ever would. But I did want real hands roaming over my body. I wanted to feel the warmth of a real dick throbbing inside me, hitting spots that even a giant dildo would miss.

Sliding on fishnets that gave me a heathenish sort of confidence, I kept my eyes on the figurine. Had I not known better, I would have sworn his gaze darkened hungrily.

"You like what you see?" I spread my legs for him to get the full view of my lacy red thong. "I bet you want a taste."

He said nothing, of course. But I felt like a damn vixen all the same.

EIGHT

THE SEVEN-INCH HEELS had been a choice. They pinched every inch and nerve in my feet, and I walked like a newborn giraffe, but this was the price I was willing to pay—especially when I saw the scandalized giddiness on Yazmine's and Katie's faces.

"Holy shit, Victoria." Yazmine dramatically cooled herself with a delicate fan. "You took the alter ego theme seriously! A compassionate nurse by day, dominatrix ready to do harm with her stethoscope by night."

"I thought dressing in your alter ego was the point," I said.

"The point is to be sexy—which you are!" Katie exclaimed. She was a sexified version of one of her favorite anime characters, the slits of her skirt traveling to dangerous heights.

"Which we *all* are," Yazmine added. She was dressed like a courtesan. Her skirts brazenly fanned out around her legs, taking up several bar seats in her orbit. With each breath, her cleavage crested over her bodice like rising dough.

Katie clapped. "This is so fun. I've cosplayed for anime conventions but never like this. It's very . . . titillating." She shimmied her small breasts.

"Damn right," Yazmine agreed. "We get to celebrate our sexiness but without any creeps around trying to hit on us." She turned her eyes to me. "Unless you *want* someone to hit on you, and if that's the case we can take these looks to the streets."

I barked a laugh. "That's the last thing I want." *Unless they could help get me off.* Nah. I didn't want to expose my body to some stranger. I also didn't want something that took effort or time away from my friends.

Thumping bass from the music playing inside the ballroom rattled the wine glasses hanging from the bar. My body moved on instinct. I'd always loved dancing. It hadn't been Alanzo's thing, and I didn't have a ton of friends that lived near me to go out clubbing with. Besides, once I became a mom, I sort of lost the energy to try. But right now, I had all the energy in the world.

"Let's go," I said. "Before these heels kill me."

Giggling, we swept into the pulsing ballroom. Colorful spotlights pirouetted on the decorated walls and fell over the dancing guests. The room was packed with attendees and authors dressed as their alter egos. Actors done up to look like famous book characters roamed about taking photos.

"This is amazing!" Katie shouted over the blaring beats coming from the DJ booth.

It was. I'd never felt so at home among strangers in my life. These were my people. *Our* people. Books were powerful in that way. The stories they wove into our hearts changed us. Made us better. They gave us community.

"I'll get us drinks!" Yazmine bellowed, pointing at the small bar. "Meet you on the dance floor!"

Katie and I bopped to reggaeton as we made our way toward the front of the room. My hips swayed. My body rolled. For the last twenty-four years, I'd only danced while cleaning the house or stiffly at receptions. I'd been too self-conscious to move the way I really wanted to with my kids sitting at the kitchen table doing homework or my husband's business partners milling around the wedding cakes.

Or Alanzo judging from afar.

But the people dancing right now were unleashing their inhibitions. A mermaid gyrated and writhed around us. Twin aliens were practically having a threesome on the dance floor with a vampire. I wanted that. Not the threesome, I don't think. I wanted to move and not care what others thought. I knew these people wouldn't care. But I also wanted to dance whether they did or not.

So I did.

I shook my tits. I dropped it low, ignoring my popping knees. I twerked as if my ass cheeks jiggling had the power to save my life. I suppose this sort of dancing, this sort of openness, *was* saving me. It was loosening the gauze I'd cinched around my heart to stop it from being too free. It kept me from laughing too hard or dancing too sexy or doing anything that I thought a mother and wife shouldn't be.

With each twirl. Each twerk. I was stripping away every lie Alanzo made me believe about myself. I deserved to feel sexy. I deserved to take up space.

Before I knew it, a circle had formed around me and Katie. Costumed attendees were cheering and whistling and shouting for us to get lower. Yazmine, who stood among the circle, balancing three drinks in her hands, was cheering hardest and loudest of them all.

The joy flooding my veins was so pure, so visceral, I almost cried. But I didn't want those tears to turn into something deeper. I didn't want them to remind me of the tears I once shed that tasted of despair.

"Get over here!" I shouted to Yazmine. Without a second of hesitation, she grooved to meet us in the center of the dance circle. She handed me a whisky sour, my favorite. Of course, she knew that. My friends knew what I liked. They knew me. They loved me for who I was and never once made me feel guilty about it. If anything, they wanted me to be *more* open with expressing myself.

Now I was.

At that very moment, I was expressing the hell out of my ass. And, holy fuck, did it feel good. More people joined in, until we were all writhing to the rhythm of our own liberation.

NINE

SEVEN-INCH HEELS DANGLING from two fingers, I swayed toward my hotel room. The icy AC nipped at the sweat still clinging to my nurse costume. I hummed and giggled. I was so thoroughly pleased with myself for shutting the party down that I didn't care if anyone was watching me from their peepholes. In fact, I wanted them to look. I wanted people to stare at the ass that could bounce like a basketball. At the boobs pushed so high up they could shelf books.

For so long, I hid my body away. I would never do that for anyone again.

Wouldn't it be nice if some hot man thrust open his door and said he wanted to dick me down right then and there?

I snorted. Who said things like *dick me down*?

But, damn, I wouldn't be mad if it happened.

I slowed when I made it to my door and peeked over my shoulder. "Anyone?" I asked into the lonely hallway burdened by baby-vomit-colored carpet. Sadly, no wannabe dick downers came to my rescue.

The lock disengaged as I tapped the keycard onto the little card reader, and I shoved the door open with a shoulder.

"Home sweet home," I whispered into the dark. Flicking on the entryway light, I teetered toward my open suitcase, flung the heels inside, and sat heavily on my bed.

The relief of being off my feet was instant. I sighed with delight and rubbed my arches. "Best night ever."

Almost.

It would have been perfect if I had someone to help me relieve the need building inside me. If only that damn vibrator hadn't thrown a fit at the airport, I'd be dicking it down right now.

I pulled off my fishnets and let them flutter to the floor. My gaze traveled to the desk where the little warrior had stood, watching me as I readied for the night. I blinked. He wasn't there. Only his small spear remained.

"What the hell?"

I checked under the bed. Then in my book cart.

Nowhere.

"This is so strange."

I flicked on the bathroom light and balked.

There he was. His little ripped body positioned to face directly toward the shower.

That shouldn't have been possible. I knew for a fact that I had left him on the desk. Hadn't I?

A giggle escaped me.

"I guess you must really want to watch me bathe."

Obviously, he didn't offer a reply.

I smirked. "Now you're quiet."

The thought of someone watching me, even if it was a four-inch doll, made me feel empowered. Alanzo never let me do little strip teases for him. He never let me lead or do what I wanted in bed. I think it was because it gave me the power. It gave me dominance. I suppose small-*minded* men couldn't handle such a thing.

Good thing he wasn't here.

This effigy, however, was about to get one hell of a show.

I bent over, exposing my thong and ass to him, and twisted on the faucet. Water cascaded from the large showerhead. I stuck my hand in the flowing spray and waited for it to warm. Fingers dripping, I faced my warrior. I ran my hand over my collarbones. Pebbles of water crawled down my chest and disappeared into my cleavage. I brought my fingers to the front zipper at the crest of my nurse corset.

"Shall I strip for you?"

I swore I saw his tiny Adam's apple bob.

Those whiskey sours had been strong as hell. I was seeing things. But I let myself pretend he was real. That he was as the artist said, some do-gooder spirit trapped inside this tiny body, waiting to find his ultimate purpose.

"I can be your purpose," I told him.

My breasts tumbled out as I slowly unzipped the costume. The polyester dress fell to the ground. My thong followed suit. As the condensation ate away at the mirror, I watched myself pull out the pins in my hair one by one, my breasts swishing with each tug.

"I bet you wish you could touch these," I teased, giving him a little shimmy. "Too bad you aren't real."

I turned my back to him, stepped into the shower, and closed the glass door. The air was luxuriously warm, but the mist fogged up my warrior's view of me.

"We don't want anything obstructing the show."

I pressed my breasts to the glass and swished them from side to side until my glistening body was on full display.

Lathering my skin, I pictured my warrior coming to life. I squeezed my breasts, pretending my small hands were replaced by a large, strong grasp. I pinched my nipples, imagining his calloused fingers were twisting and toying with them.

I groaned at the sensation—at the thought of being wanted.

But it wasn't enough. I needed friction. I needed hard flesh slapping against my clit.

I brought my hand down to my silky folds and grinded against it. I stuck two fingers inside and moaned, "I wish this was you."

The sound of something falling jerked my attention toward the counter. My little warrior had tumbled on his side. His jaguar headpiece slid into the sink.

My brows furrowed. He'd been standing securely moments ago.

His small body twitched.

"What the fuck?"

I sprang out of the shower to get a better look. That's when I noticed something had been inscribed at the base of the figurine.

Lick me.

"Lick me?" I suddenly remembered the note left under the table.

Now you can bring the book boyfriend of your dreams to life.

Directions: For a lover so remarkable you'd swear he was pulled right out of a fairy tale, simply give this effigy a lick.

I'd heard of kissing frogs in search of a prince. But in this case, it was more like: lick this little warrior if you want some dick.

I laughed. "This is absurd."

I stood the warrior back up and started for the shower. My body was squeaky clean, but I wasn't paying for this water bill, and if I couldn't get myself off, then languishing on the shower bench and letting the warm spray wash over me would have to do.

Something thudded on the counter again.

I peeked over my shoulder.

My warrior had toppled once more. This time his loincloth had fallen to the side, and his dick was sticking straight up.

"Goodness." The detail on it was impressive. I could see every ridge and vein.

Like what you see? a deep voice cooed.

I screamed and stumbled back, bumping into the toilet.

"What sort of toy had that woman given me?"

Lick me and you will soon find out, his voice caressed my ear.

Wait. This wasn't just any toy, this must be a sexy toy. I laughed at my sudden realization. No wonder the reviews were so great.

Lick me, Victoria.

A shudder ran through me. My nipples swelled at the bass in his tone.

With a what-the-hell sigh, I picked him up. The familiar firm, yet fleshy feel of him called to me. I realized I wasn't just curious. I *wanted* to lick him. I wanted to taste him.

I brought the effigy to my mouth. My tongue grazed over his

dick. I swear it pulsed. I pulled back, balking, but my hunger for him was stronger than my confusion. I pressed my tongue against his rippling abs. He tasted of salt and earth. Tasted deliciously human. As I languidly licked him from bottom to top, I heard a gratified moan.

TEN

NOTHING HAPPENED.

My warrior was still just a figurine.

Rolling my eyes, I placed him back down on the counter. Did I really expect anything else? I appraised his naked form. His perfectly sculpted dick. What a shame for it to go to waste.

Maybe he needed to be licked harder? Like a lollipop.

"Just get in the shower, Victoria," I told myself.

But then, my warrior began to vibrate. His little body rocked back and forth—a buzzing noise emanating from inside him. Just like my dildo but louder, greedier for my attention. Well, he had all my attention now.

The figurine started to grow.

My jaw dropped.

The warrior lengthened and widened. Lengthened and widened. Lengthened and widened—until I had to cock my head back just to look into his eyes.

I stood there, panting so hard my heart could have given out. There was a full-grown toy man inside my bathroom.

How could this be? What sort of strange mechanics could make something like this possible?

Besides his mannequin-like stance, there was nothing toyish about him. He looked so real. His chest was broad and hairless, covered in beautiful markings from an ancient world. His abs were taut and the V at the base of his torso led to the thickest dick I'd ever laid eyes on in real life. It was semi-hard, and I had to fight the urge to take it in my grasp just to see how it felt.

But why should I hold myself back? This toy was mine, wasn't it? He had supposedly "chosen me." The reviews on the website had been stellar. I guess I could see why if all the figurines were as beautiful as my warrior.

I reached for him but stopped. I knew it was ridiculous, but I also knew what it felt like to be someone's possession. The thought of grabbing this big, beautiful dick without the warrior's permission, without knowing this was what he wanted, felt wrong.

My hands fell at my sides.

Touch me, Victoria. Please.

I blinked up at him. "How are you talking?"

His lips didn't move. My eyes flicked to the foggy mirror which offered me a glimpse of his beautiful backside. I didn't see a speaker or voice box there.

I want you to touch me, Victoria, he purred. *Feel my cock. I know you want to.*

There was no explaining how that artist could have created this giant growing toy, but I was beyond trying to understand. I wanted to feel his soft skin on my palms. *He* wanted me to feel him. That was all the permission I needed.

Timidly, I sauntered through the mist filling the bathroom. The shower water hissed against the tile. But I didn't hear it. I didn't smell the fruity soap. Or feel the heat nipping at my cheeks. All my attention was zeroed in on him. The pads of my fingers grazed over the tip of his dick. His cock twitched before growing harder.

My eyes widened. "Can you actually move?"

Do you want me to?

"I do."

I wrapped both hands around the shaft and squeezed. A soft groan filled my ears. My clit swelled as I stroked him. His dick grew harder with each rise and fall, and a giddy thrill ran through me. Look what my hands alone could do. Imagine how hard my mouth would make him. I got down on my knees and licked him like a lollipop. I took his head in my mouth and swirled my tongue across his hole.

Fuck, Victoria, he groaned. *Fuck, you feel so good.*

His body shifted, deepening inside my mouth. I took him in. His moans alone made me want to taste him in the back of my throat.

"Wait, my queen." A hand grazed over my hair. My eyes shot up, and I met my warrior's heated gaze. A rosy flush peeked through his brown skin. He smiled.

His lips actually moved. I yelped and scrambled back, my very naked ass thumping into the shower door. He's real?

"Hello, Victoria, my queen."

His voice, his smile, his sexy dick, it all stirred me into a frenzy. I took hold of the base of his shaft, ready to give him the head of his life, but he gently pulled out of my mouth. I pouted as he dropped to one knee. His long hair fell over his shoulders and curtained between us, but his eyes never left mine.

"Who are you?" I whispered.

"My name is Ollin," he said. "I have fought through death and time to meet you here, Victoria."

I gaped at him in wonder. "Did my friends put you and the artist up to this? Like . . . is this something they paid for?"

He smiled warmly. "Our meeting was orchestrated by the goddesses."

I giggled. I always did that when I was too overwhelmed to say anything rational. Alanzo hated it. Which made me hate that about myself in return. But Ollin simply looked at me with understanding.

"Why would the goddesses bring you to me? Doesn't seem like something they'd care about."

"Nonsense. Your needs matter."

Tell that to my ex.

"I was alive once, long ago. I served my Queen regnant, Tlapalizquixochtzin, until the bitter end. I fought through fire and flame, through hundreds of men to keep her safe from the colonizers. As we lay dying, she made me vow to her that I would come back to this world, if given a chance, that I would stand and fight for another woman until she reclaimed her own power." He placed his hand on my arm. Lust tore through me. "The universe has given me that chance. It is your time to reclaim your power, Victoria Lopez."

I balked. "My power?"

"There is nothing greater than a woman who believes in herself. A woman who knows what she is worth. Tonight, I will remind you that your voice, your desires, your wants should never be diminished. I am here to make you believe in your prowess, my queen."

"And how will you do that?"

"By making you come."

My jaw dropped.

Maybe this was all some wildly vivid dream. Maybe I'd fallen and cracked my head, and I was passed out. Whatever the case, I wasn't going to let this opportunity go. I'd had his dick in my hands, in my mouth, I knew how smooth and delicious it was. I wanted to know how it felt thrust deep inside me. Reborn warrior, toy, or whatever the hell he was. I wanted him to fuck me sideways.

"What should we do first, Ollin?"

His eyes bore into me, practically fucking me already. "Whatever you wish. You are wholly in charge, my queen."

Whatever I wished? For the first time in twenty-four years, someone wanted me to do whatever I wanted. I gulped. What did I want?

Still on his knees, Ollin watched me. Waited for me. His tongue moistened his lips. I smirked. I knew exactly what that tongue could do.

Pretending as if I were as queenly as he believed me to be, I stood. I walked around him and popped myself onto the vanity counter. "I want you to taste me." I spread myself wide for him.

He crawled to me like the jaguar stitched on his discarded loincloth. A low growl emanated from his throat. "I've wanted to taste you since I first saw you. And when you dressed before me earlier tonight, and you were teasing me with those lacy underthings, I almost went mad with hunger for you."

My cheeks flamed. I should be horrified. But I was too busy panting with anticipation.

Ollin's large and calloused fingers glided up my ankles, over my calves and thighs. I was throbbing for him. One of his thumbs grazed over my clit, and I gasped. For the last few years, I had wondered what it would be like when someone new touched me. I wondered if it would feel awkward or wrong or if it would blow my mind. He rubbed against my most sensitive spot. His other hand clenched around my breast and squeezed.

I bucked into his grasp.

I guess I found my answer. My mind and body were officially blown.

"Yes," he whispered into my delicate flesh. "I want you to see the stars tonight, for you shine brighter than they."

His tongue slid up my folds.

I clamped my lips together to seal in my shocked cry. I grabbed his hair and spread my legs wider, opening for him so he could devour every part of me.

"How is this real?" I gasped.

His hands tugged and pinched my nipples while his tongue flicked over my clit. My bud swelled. My entire body flexed.

"That's it, my queen. Come for me. Let yourself be free."

Two fingers thrust into me while his thumb and tongue worked me in other places. I gritted my teeth. I only knew how to be quiet during sex.

"You're holding back. I can sense it. Scream if you want. Do whatever you desire. You deserve this. You need this."

He was absolutely right.

And as he continued banging me with his mouth and fingers, I came. I came so hard and for so long that I truly did see the stars.

ELEVEN

I DIDN'T SCREAM.

I howled.

I bellowed.

I became undone and then pieced myself back together again. I had just orgasmed for the first time in far too long, and it was fucking fantastic. But it only made me hungrier for more.

My eyes found his. Face slick with sweat and . . . me, he was sexy as hell.

I panted, "Are you really real?"

"As real as you want me to be. I'm here to serve you in any capacity until you no longer need me." He stood to his full height and pressed his body between my thighs. After something so intimate, I usually ran to clean myself off, to dress and move on with my day, but I didn't want that. I wanted to stay in my nakedness. To enjoy the way his eyes trailed over every part of me.

"What if I always need you?" I asked.

"Then I will be here."

"How am I supposed to bring some six-foot sex spirit onboard my flight home?"

Laughter rumbled deep in his chest. "Do you remember the name of the booth where you found me?"

"BookCon Carry-On?"

He nodded. His large hands kneaded my thighs. God, it felt good.

"I will return to my clay nature whenever you need. Simply wish me goodnight, and I will reform as I came."

"You're kidding."

"I am not."

His hands found their way to my shoulders. His thumbs dug into my knots. "Keep doing that and I might come again. It's been years since someone touched me like this."

"This is how you should be treated always. You must never settle. Never put your needs last ever again. I am here to make sure you remember that."

His fingers moved to my scalp, and he massaged my head like a sculptor working clay. I closed my eyes and moaned. I never thought I'd want a man back in my life, but someone to care for me, someone to make me feel like this, like a goddamn queen, would be nice.

Ollin continued to work his magic on me. His skilled fingers rediscovered places I'd forgotten needed attention. When he found his way to my ass and squeezed my soft cheeks, a pulse of heat spurred inside my core. I let my head fall back, exposing my neck and chest to him. He took my breasts in his strong grasp.

"Aren't you upset a man like you didn't come back to help someone important?"

"You *are* important."

"No. I mean, like a warrior?"

He bent down and kissed me under my jaw. "You are a warrior. To live in this world, in this timeline, is no easy feat.

There's nowhere else I'd rather be than here with you for as long as you need me."

"It doesn't feel right to just use you for sex." I wouldn't ever want anyone to feel like Alanzo made me feel.

"Consider me your whetstone. I am here to sharpen you for battle. Whatever that may be. I do not feel used, Victoria. I feel invigorated. Trust me, I will enjoy every second of this," he whispered into my ear.

Chills rippled over my body.

His dick was already growing with anticipation.

"You'll do whatever I wish, huh?" I asked.

"I will."

I smiled. "Good."

TWELVE

OLLIN'S glorious dick was a thing of beauty—so large and thick. And it was hard for me. I wanted it harder.

"Step back," I ordered.

"That's right. Bask in your authority."

My warrior did as I asked.

"Touch yourself," I commanded.

His eyes did not leave mine when he spit into his palm. Nor did they break our stare when he slid his clenched fist up and down that long shaft.

"How does that feel?" I asked.

"Achingly good." He stroked himself in languid thrusts. "But you will feel better."

"You think so?" I brought my hands up to my breasts and squeezed them. I toyed with my nipples and watched his erection grow harder. "Oh, you're right. I *do* feel good."

He bit his bottom lip. Not in the coy, sexy sort of way. His teeth clamped onto it as if it were a lifeline. As if he were trying to pierce his skin to distract himself from cumming all over the bathroom floor.

I tugged at my nipples and asked, "Do you like what you see?"

"You're more breathtaking than a thousand sunsets."

"Want to feel what it's like to be inside me?"

"More than I long to breathe."

I shoved myself off the counter, bent over, and licked his tip. His head fell back, and he moaned as if he were in agony.

This was so much fun. Torturing this man with my body, with my mouth, made me feel like the queen he claimed I was.

I turned off the shower and stood before him. He was so much taller than me. His body toned, his thighs powerful. I couldn't wait to feel the force of them as he pounded into me.

"Follow me," I commanded.

He grinned. "I'll follow you anywhere."

I ushered him out of the bathroom and shoved him onto the bed. His body bounced on the buoyant mattress, his dick swinging back and forth. His mouth fell open in shock. Either he'd never been on a cushion so soft, or he'd never been dominated like this before. Based on the way the corners of his lips quirked up, he loved whatever was happening to him.

I crawled onto the bed, running my fingers over his legs as I crept over his body. He wasn't very hairy, which was fine by me. It was easier for me to take in every firm cut of his muscles. I slid my tongue up the base of his dick. He clutched the blankets, and his abs went taut.

"Stars above, Victoria," he growled.

The sound of a man finding my mouth worthy, of him bucking and writhing at my mere touch made me even wetter than I already was. I straddled him. Nuzzling his dick between my slick folds. I toyed with his tip, rubbing his precum around in circles while I grinded against him.

His jaw unclenched, and he rasped, "You are going to be the end of me."

"Should I stop?" I teased.

"You should do whatever you want, my queen."

That was exactly what I wanted to hear. I was his queen. I wanted him to cry out my name—to worship me like I deserved.

I was on the pill. I doubted this reborn warrior could impregnate me anyway. But stranger things had happened, like a hand-carved warrior coming to life to dick me down.

"Before we do this, have you . . . are you . . ." I had never had to ask someone if they had STDs before. I know I was his 'purpose,' but I had to be cautious nonetheless.

"My body has remained untouched for centuries. I am wholly yours. Now, please." His voice came out harsh. I was grinding against him too well.

I lifted myself up and seated my opening against his tip. My breasts swung in his face, and he took the opportunity to lift his head up and swipe his tongue over each nipple. I groaned in delight.

"You taste so good, Victoria." His hand clutched one of my breasts. He squeezed. "You feel so good."

My pussy pulsed for him. I couldn't hold off any longer.

Slowly, achingly, I eased myself down upon him. My opening stretched around him. Pain and pure, ecstatic pleasure rocked through me. I didn't hold back my cries of lust. I let everything out as I slid up and down his length, lubricating his shaft until finally, finally I had taken all of him in.

We both sighed in relief.

He filled me so completely, hitting every nerve in my core. He squeezed my breast again. His thumb flicked over my nipple.

Slowly, I grinded against him. I buried his dick deeper inside me. I wanted to feel more of him—every last morsel of his flesh.

My pace quickened. His hands slid to my ass and pressed me harder against him as I rode him with fervor. This was it! This was everything I'd been missing in my life. This pure, beautiful power.

He cried out. Never had a man been so consumed by my actions. So what if he wasn't from this time? So what he'd been reborn into an effigy? He was here, and he wanted me, and I deserved this. I deserved to be craved and chosen and fucked.

I deserved to fuck—to ride a man until his eyes rolled back in his head.

That was exactly what I did.

My body slapped harder against his. The fullness of him. The way my clit ground so perfectly against him sent me barreling close to the edge. I rode him harder. Faster. Like I was chasing the orgasm that had been kept away from me for so excruciatingly long.

He grunted. I knew he was close to cumming inside me. I wanted it. I craved it. His jaw clenched as I fucked him.

His dick throbbed inside me. "Vic-tor-i-a," he growled.

I'd never heard anyone indulge in every syllable and letter in my name like that before. He said it like a plea, like he was begging for me to save him. I was ready to answer his prayers.

"Call my name," I commanded. "Scream for me, Ollin."

As we pounded into each other he cried out, "Fuck, Victoria. Fuck, you feel so good!"

An orgasm tore through me. It was so strong, so miraculous

that I shook in brazen release. I screamed his name again and again, and I smiled as he screamed mine.

THIRTEEN

I LAY DRAPED over Ollin's broad chest for a few minutes while I caught my breath. His strong arms were snug around my body, and his warm dick was still inside me. To my surprise, I was ready for him again.

This reminded me of my favorite book *Warrior Lovers*. The FMC was a badass warrior. After she was captured by an enemy clan, she found herself in the clutches of the super sexy new leader of the warrior clan. Her death would prove his strength as leader. Despite their circumstances, they fell for each other, and they secretly banged whenever they could sneak away at night. When I first read it, I remembered thinking, there's no way a woman would want this much sex. But now I got it.

I too wanted to sneak off with Ollin and fuck under the stars.

Ollin chuckled.

I lifted my head. "What's so funny?"

He grinned. "I can feel your need building."

"Is that right?"

To prove his point, he gently thrust his hips upward, making my clit quiver in response.

"You mentioned wanting me to see the stars," I said. "I have an idea."

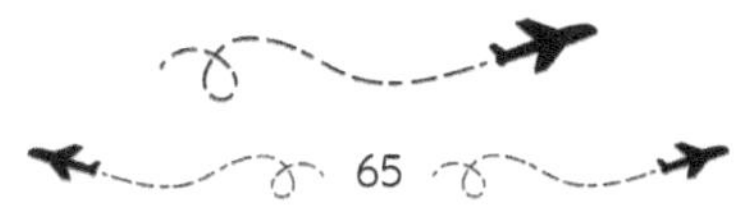

WRAPPED in robes and nothing else, Ollin and I snuck onto the hotel roof. Since the rooftop bar had been closed for refurbishment, I hoped no one would be around. Thank the goddesses, I had been right. Save for the stars winking down at us, we were wonderfully alone.

Only one other hotel towered over us, but it was dark enough that no one would see us.

Ollin swooped me up in his arms. I yelped and giggled as he carried me toward a lounge chair at the center of the rooftop. He put me on my feet and tore off his robe. His long hair fluttered in the breeze. My nipples hardened and I shivered, but I knew he'd heat me up soon enough.

He placed his robe over the lounge chair. Bowing, he gestured toward the chair and said, "Your throne, my queen."

Smiling, I unloosed my belt and let my breasts swell out of my robe. Languidly, I sat on the chair and leaned back, opening my legs to him.

Ollin licked his long fingers before sliding them over my folds. He slipped his fingers inside me and moaned. "You're so wet."

He pulled his fingers out and slid my juices down his rock-hard shaft.

His free hand grabbed one of my legs, and he placed it over his shoulder. As he masturbated, he rubbed the tip of his dick up and down my folds. My fingers squeezed around the side of the chair.

"What do you want, my queen?" he whispered. "What do you want me to do to you?"

I panted. "I want you to fuck me under the stars."

Ollin smirked, then slid his dick inside me.

This new position stretched me further. I didn't hold back my moans of pleasure.

His thrusts were slow at first. Teasing. He moved himself up and down, up and down, while his thumb toyed with my clit. He bent down and sucked on my bottom lip. I almost came then and there, but then he slid his dick all the way to the base, filling me completely. I gasped, and he pinned his lips against mine, devouring my lusty moans.

"Fuck me," I growled into his mouth.

As our tongues met, Ollin drove into me with the power of those muscular thighs. He slapped against my throbbing pussy, nailing me against my makeshift throne. The metal legs of the lounge chair scraped against the cement rooftop. Our bodies clapped together in perfect harmony. I cried out. I shouted his name. I clawed at his skin.

"Harder," I ordered. "Harder!"

Ollin did exactly what he was told.

He sucked and plucked and toyed with every inch of my body, and he fucked me hard under the stars.

FOURTEEN

WE RETURNED to my room and fucked each other again. And again. He dicked me down in every position, every spot we could come up with. But all those years of built-up tension could not be satiated. I wasn't sure if I'd ever stop wanting him inside me, wanting his tongue and fingers finding new spots to explore.

We didn't talk. There wasn't time for that, and that wasn't why he'd found me. My warrior knew what he was there for—to remind me that I deserved every good thing in the world. I deserved to be worshiped in body and in spirit.

When the sun peeked through the curtains, I brought him back into the bathroom. And I rode him on the shower bench as he massaged shampoo into my hair.

FIFTEEN

OLLIN WATCHED me as I readied myself for the final day of Flirty Flings BookCon. I made sure to stay naked until the last minute just so his eyes could feast. But I knew the girls would be coming to find me any minute now. I shimmied on my skirt and pulled on my sports bra. Ollin handed me my shirt.

His fingers grazed against mine, and my skin heated. I bit my lip. Maybe we had time for a quicky. Ollin's mouth quirked into a grin when I pulled his naked body close to me. I brought his hand under my skirt and pushed my underwear to the side. His fingers found my opening at once.

We both groaned at my wet and hungry pussy.

But just as his first thrusts began to make me soar, frantic knocks banged on the hotel door.

Katie called, "Wakie, wakie!"

"We've got coffee," Yazmine added.

I disregarded them. I grinded against Ollin. "Don't stop. Don't you dare."

"Where's the keycard she gave you?" I heard Yazmine say to Katie.

Dammit.

Ollin pulled out his fingers.

"No," I whined.

He lapped up my juices glistening on his fingers. "I'll be here whenever you're ready."

I pouted. "You promise?"

"I do."

The card reader chimed, and the lock disengaged.

"Goodnight," I said, and Ollin's beautiful body shrunk in seconds. I scooped him from the floor and placed him on the desk just before my girls stormed in.

I whirled around, panting and still slick from Ollin's ministrations.

"Sorry," I said. "I must not have heard you. I was . . ." *getting finger banged into oblivion.* ". . .exercising." I tugged on my shirt.

Yazmine's eyes scrutinized me and then my room. The tangled sheets. The pillows flung in odd corners. Autographed books lying open-faced on the floor. She sniffed at the air. Her gaze narrowed before a creeping grin brightened her gorgeous face.

"Are you ready for another great day?" Katie asked. She grabbed the coffee from Yazmine's grasp and thrust it toward me.

I took it, smiling. I *was* ready for a great day and an even greater night.

"I am," I said. "But first, I want to go back to BookCon Carry-On."

"Oh? How come?" Katie asked.

Yazmine's attention turned to me. "Yeah. How come?"

I flicked my hair back. "I want to thank that artist for leaving me the warrior."

Drinking my coffee, I sauntered out of my room. I let my hips shake with each step. Let my shoulders roll back, exposing my wonderfully large breasts so everyone walking by could enjoy the curves of my body.

"Something is different about you," Yazmine said.

"It's true. You look like a damn boss," Katie added.

"I feel like one." I felt like I could rule the world, and all because Ollin reminded me that I should never dull my shine. Never shy away from doing and saying whatever the fuck I wanted. Because that was what I deserved.

Thanks to my dick-down warrior, I recognized my worth. I was smart, capable, a goddamn queen. I'd never set aside my crown again for any man. But I might spread my legs for him.

"Hurry up, girls," I said. "I want to see if that artist has any special figurines for you, too."

ACKNOWLEDGMENTS

The last time I went to a romance book convention, I walked around the room and smiled at all the deliciously salacious art prints and book covers I laid eyes on. A funny thought occurred to me then. What if the six-foot-tall rabbit shifter in the book I purchased really did come to life—what if any of the characters in any of these gorgeous stories came to life? That's when the idea for *BookCon Carry-On* was born.

So, first, I'd like to thank book conventions. I'd like to thank the authors and vendors that fill the venue and the readers who are ecstatic to be there. Magic becomes real at book cons.

Thank you to the amazing team at Tides Collide Publishing. Robin Alvarez, you are a generational talent. Truly, you are so creative. The cover you put together is one of my favorite covers of all time. Thank you for listening to my wild idea and saying, "Let's do this!" I adore your enthusiasm and your tenacity.

Thank you to our amazing street team for sharing in our enthusiasm for this novella!

To Melanie Schubert: You already know how I feel about you.

To Angela Montoya: You're ok.

Huge thank you to my critique partners, Kerrie Faye and Honey Hazzard. Without your suggestions, this novella wouldn't be what it is today. I knew you would have keen eyes because you both write so incredibly well.

To Vera Valentine and M.L. Eliza and Holly Wilde, thank you for writing the stories that bring me so much joy.
Monty Amor

ABOUT THE AUTHOR

Monty Amor is a lion tamer, rocket scientist, deep-sea diver, and devoted world wanderer. When she isn't nursing baby giraffes back to health, you can find her curled beside a crackling campfire, weaving stories as warm and wild as her adventures.

instagram.com/monty_amor_author